Come Back Lily Lightly

adapted by Nora Pelizzari

from the animated movie *A Very Pony Place*

HarperFestival®

A Division of HarperCollins *Publishers*

The unicorns gathered in front of Rainbow Castle.
Lily Lightly addressed the excited crowd.
"As you all know, it's time for the
Rainbow Lights Party," she called.
"We need your help to make Unicornia shine!"

With everyone working together,
Unicornia was soon aglow with lights.
Cheerilee made another announcement.
"Lily, for all of your hard work, we bestow upon you the title
of Lily Lightly, Princess of All That Twinkles and Glows."

The unicorns cheered. Lily Lightly was very excited to
receive such an honor. In fact, she was so happy,
her horn started to glow.
Lily Lightly gasped. Had anyone seen it?

"Wow!" said Rarity. "Look at Lily's horn!"
"Oh, no!" Lily Lightly cried, horribly embarrassed.
She ran away before anyone could stop her,
and disappeared into the forest.

Meanwhile, Minty and Pinkie Pie were traveling to the
Rainbow Lights Party in a hot air balloon,
but they couldn't find Unicornia.
"Minty, look!" cried Pinkie Pie. "Let's aim for that light!"
"Good idea, Pinkie!" Minty replied. "Hold on tight!"

Below them, Brights Brightly and Rarity were searching
in the forest for Lily Lightly, but they weren't having any luck.
"She could be anywhere," Brights Brightly said.
"I wish she hadn't run away. Her horn is different, but we all like it!"

The ponies landed on the ground next to Brights Brightly
and Rarity. After saying hello, the unicorns explained
that they were looking for their missing friend.
"We saw a light right over there,"
Minty said, pointing to the bushes.

Lily Lightly was hiding behind a rock, away from her friends.
The other unicorns' horns never lit up like hers did.
She didn't like being so different from everyone else.
Suddenly, she heard a noise. Her friends had found her!

"Lily, please come out," Rarity called. "You don't have to hide.
Your horn is what makes you special."
Minty and Pinkie Pie added, "Your bright light
saved us from getting lost out here!"
"Really?" asked Lily Lightly. Her horn glowed
even more brightly . . . and it was beautiful!

When the ponies and the unicorns returned to the
Rainbow Lights Party, Lily Lightly was surprised to see that
all of the unicorns had wrapped their horns in glowing lights.
They looked just like her!

Lily Lightly was so happy, her horn glowed like the brightest star.
"Thank you all. I've learned that I should just be myself,
because what makes me different also makes me special.
Shine on, everyone!"

Positively Pink

It was early in the morning, but Minty hurried to check the birthday
book. Whose birthday was next? When she opened the book,
she saw that today's page was decorated entirely in pink.

All that pink could only mean one thing!
Minty ran through Ponyville, alerting everyone that it was
Pinkie Pie's birthday. All of the ponies sprang into action.

Puzzlemint's job was important . . . she had to keep the birthday pony from seeing the preparations for the surprise party. She looked carefully to make sure Pinkie Pie was nowhere around.

The coast was clear.
Puzzlemint ran around a corner, and . . . *crash!*
There was Pinkie Pie!

Puzzlemint thought fast. "Let's go on a puzzle hunt, Pinkie,"
she said. "The first one to find all the clues wins!"
"Oh, what fun!" exclaimed Pinkie Pie.
"We'd better get started!"

While Puzzlemint kept Pinkie Pie busy with the puzzle hunt, the rest of the ponies were turning Ponyville into a pink wonderland.

"More pink!" cried Minty. She was covered in pink paint. "Pink streamers, pink paint, pink flowers, and pink rainbows! Anything goes, as long as it's pink!"

As Pinkie Pie and Puzzlemint turned the corner into Ponyville,
Pinkie Pie gasped at the transformation.
All at once, the ponies stepped out from their hiding places.
"SURPRISE!" they cried, and started to sing the birthday song.

"Is this for me?" asked Pinkie Pie. "But it's not my birthday."

"What?" cried Minty.

Pinkie Pie smiled and said,

"Minty, my birthday is tomorrow. You must have looked at the wrong day in the birthday book!"

"What are we going to do?" asked Minty sadly.
Puzzlemint had the answer. "Since everything is ready,
let's celebrate today *and* tomorrow!"
All of the ponies thought that was a terrific idea.

"Two birthdays?" said Pinkie Pie. "Thanks, everyone!"
Rainbow Dash looked worried. "But how will we make Pinkie's
real birthday even more special?" she asked.
Minty gave both ponies a hug and said,
"With more pink, of course!"